ZORINA BALLERINA

ENZO GIANNINI

Simon & Schuster Books for Young Readers

Published by Simon & Schuster

New York · London · Toronto · Sydney · Tokyo · Singapore

SIMON & SCHUSTER BOOKS FOR YOUNG READERS
Simon & Schuster Building, Rockefeller Center, 1230 Avenue of the Americas
New York, New York 10020. Copyright © 1993 by Enzo Giannini. All rights reserved
including the right of reproduction in whole or in part in any form.
SIMON & SCHUSTER BOOKS FOR YOUNG READERS is a trademark of Simon & Schuster.
The text for this book was set in 16 pt. Kennerly. The illustrations were
done in watercolor and colored pencil.
Manufactured in the United States of America

10 9 8 7 6 5 4 3 2 1

Library of Congress Cataloging-in-Publication Data
Giannini, Enzo. Zorina ballerina / by Enzo Giannini.
Summary: A little elephant named Zorina gets her
chance to be a circus star.   [1. Elephants—Fiction.
2. Dancing—Fiction.]   I. Giannini, Enzo, ill.   II. Title.
PZ7.P44454Zo   1992   [E]—dc20   CIP   91-21970
ISBN 0-671-74776-2

To Pam, who had the idea —EG

Once upon a time there was a little elephant named Zorina. She and her family were part of the biggest circus in the world.

One day Red Hot the clown told Zorina and her mother, "You elephants are going to get your big chance to become stars."

But Red Hot was gone before Zorina could ask what he meant.

The next day a famous ballet master arrived
to teach the elephants to polka.

"It's the great Balanchine," whispered the
elephants.

He was from Russia and was very elegant. His
friend Maestro Stravinsky came to write special
music for the elephants.

Zorina imagined the glamorous life of a prima ballerina, elephant-style.

Each elephant was to have a pink ballet skirt, a headdress made of bells and feathers, and big dangly gold earrings.

"Mama, I want to polka, too," said Zorina.
"I'm not sure," said her mother. "I think you might be a little young to perform."

Modoc was the star of the elephant ballet.
The only thing she enjoyed more than dancing
was eating peanuts.

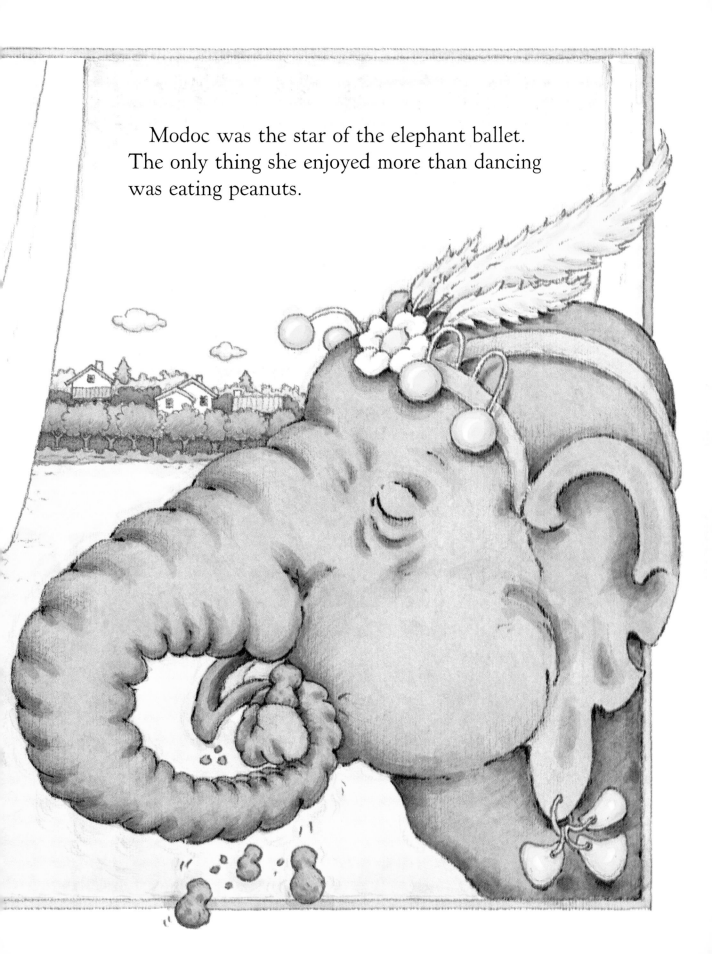

Zorina watched the rehearsals and imagined what it would be like to dance under the big top. She tapped her tail to Maestro Stravinsky's music.

The clowns knew Zorina longed to dance. "We'll teach you to polka, Zorina," they said. And they did.

Everyone contributed a handkerchief to make a ballet skirt for Zorina. Red Hot, Claudine, and Joey played the music as Zorina swayed and thumped, twirled and bumped—with Coco the clown for a partner.

Zorina loved to polka!

One afternoon Joey announced, "Big news! Modoc is sick. She ate too many peanuts and can't perform tonight!"

"This is Zorina's big chance," said Claudine, and the clowns began to plan.

Zorina was thrilled as she put on her headdress and gold earrings.

Joey told Gus, the old spotlight man, about the change in plans, and Red Hot got a caravan of clown cars to transport Zorina, hidden in a bouquet of balloons.

At last the moment had come. Zorina could hardly believe it was really happening.

"And now, ladies and gentlemen, children of all ages," boomed the ringmaster, "our Elephant Extravaganza. Watch these bounteous ballerinas as they dance for you the Circus Polka!"

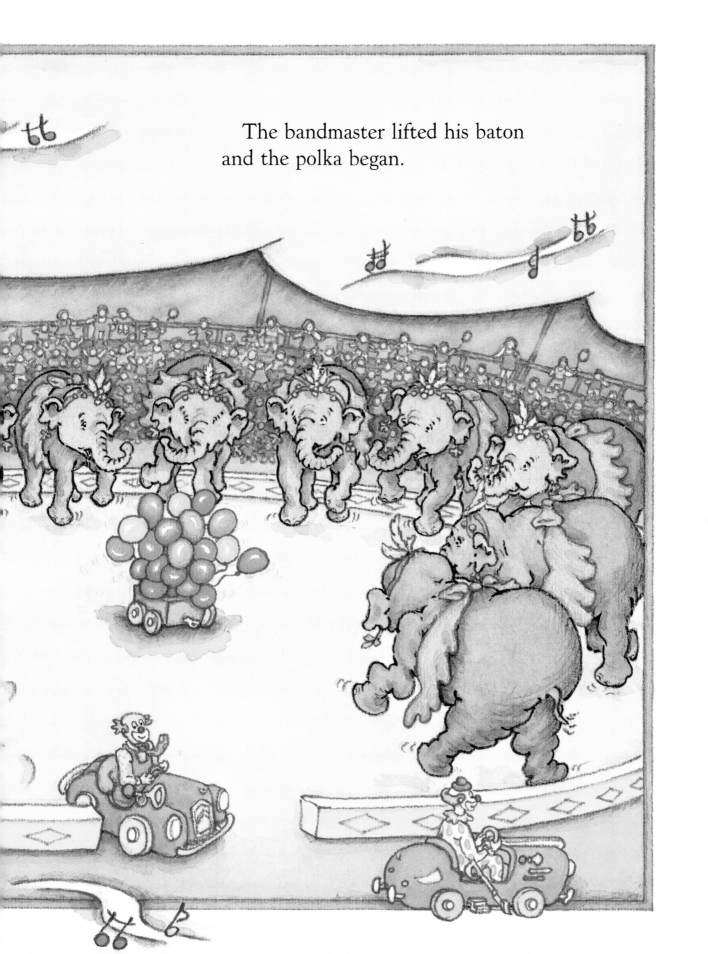

The bandmaster lifted his baton
and the polka began.

Gus turned the spotlight on the center ring. Up,
up rose the balloons, and there was Zorina swaying
to the music.

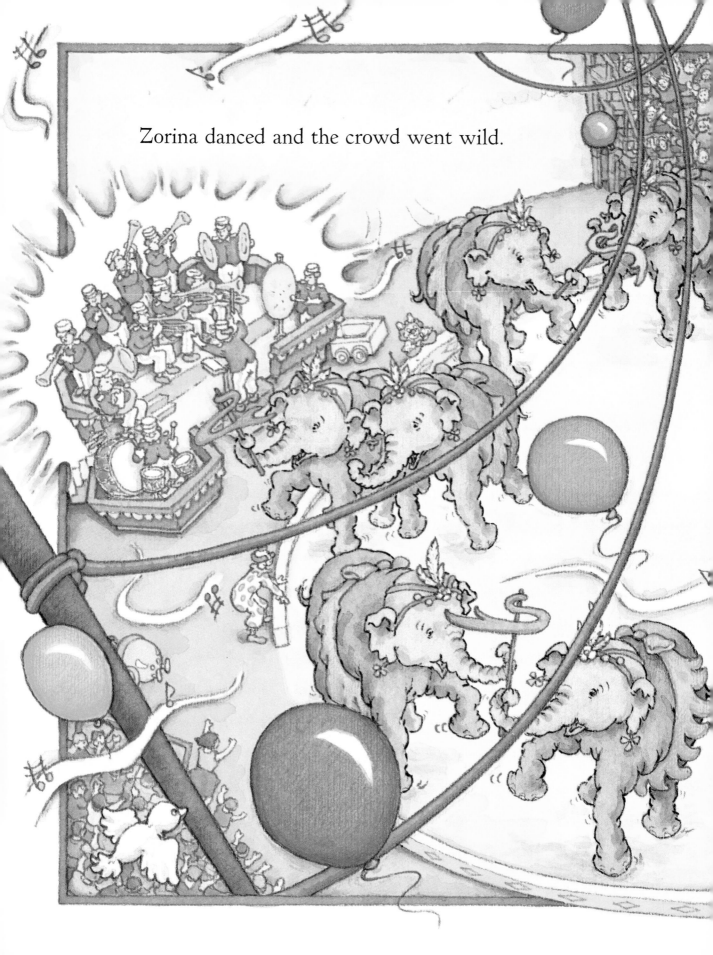

Zorina danced and the crowd went wild.

She was indeed a star.

A NOTE TO THE READER

The elephants did polka—fifty of them, all in pink, on April 9, 1942, at New York's Madison Square Garden, and for more than 245 performances thereafter of the Ringling Brothers and Barnum & Bailey Circus. The star was Modoc, the only elephant in history known to do the black bottom. Famous Russian ballet master George Balanchine choreographed *The Elephant Ballet.* He asked his friend Igor Stravinsky to compose special music. Stravinsky dedicated his "The Circus Polka" to "a young elephant."

On June 21, 1972, "The Circus Polka" premiered with fifty-four children from the School of American Ballet, and Jerome Robbins as ringmaster. It has since become a classic for very young dancers.

Enzo Giannini